The Mystery of the Shrine Beneath

THE MYSTERY OF THE SHRINE BENEATH

ANNE R. HUGHES

iUniverse, Inc.
Bloomington

The Mystery of the Shrine Beneath

iUniverse books may be ordered through booksellers or by contacting:

iUniverse
1663 Liberty Drive
Bloomington, IN 47403
www.iuniverse.com
1-800-Authors (1-800-288-4677)

ISBN: 978-1-4759-5843-0 (sc)
ISBN: 978-1-4759-5844-7 (ebk)

Printed in the United States of America

iUniverse rev. date: 11/15/2012

Contents

Dedication

This book is dedicated to my dear friend Gail Goldberg and my son Matt Hughes. These two individuals have believed in me when life threw its toughest storms.

A Note From Anne

This book has been an effort of much love and hours of hard work. There are many that I would like to thank for their love, prayers, and support.

My son, Matt who grew up in Thomson, Georgia and is a great artist is always an inspiration to me. He has offered much support to his mother throughout all of my books as he was illustrator for the first three books.

My editor, Laura Roberts, is like a daughter to me and has done a magnificent job.

I owe much to my sisters Jean Eickhoff and Sue Tetterton and their families who always offer valuable support.

A special thank you goes to my dear friend Gail Goldberg who funded this book. I am also thankful to her dog Biscuit who visits me on a regular basis.

Many thanks go to the staff and residents of Budd Terrace and to Palmer and her special dogs.

For spiritual support, Diana and Jim Roberts, Megan Brown, and Anne Allen, I am grateful. Thanks to Jim for the special angel that you drew for this book.

I am also grateful for several special individuals Suzy Jennings, Betty Williams, Valerie Williams, Bernice Munroe, Tom Munroe, Beverly Willingham, Alicia Starr, Jean Robertson, Robert Kohler, Glen Robertson, Minnie Foster, Ruth DeLoach, Susan Snyder, D. C. Hughes, Donna Heinz-Myerick, Nina Harrison, Virginia Knox, Kenya Engram, Zachary Kramer, Virginia Vaughn, and Susan Harris-Snyder.

Last but not least I want to thank my special lion, Max Cleland who has lifted me up time after time when I feel I cannot go on. To him I owe much.

Foreword

What can be said about Mrs. Anne Hughes that is not already seen in her amazing spirit? Have you ever met someone for the first time and felt like you have known them forever? Though I have only had the privilege of knowing Anne Hughes for only a year, it seems like our unique friendship is one that has been around for years.

If you would ever have the pleasure to meet Anne Hughes, you would almost always find her busy. A true example of one who knows that there is always work to be done, Anne Hughes has found her life's work in inspiring others to live lives full of joy, love, peace, full of the simple pleasures in life, and full of God's grace. This is true in every interaction that Anne Hughes and I have had. Even if my frequent visits are only just to stop and say hi, no matter how busy she may be, she always finds the time to stop whatever it is that she is doing just to welcome you in! Somehow she always manages to focus each visit on you rather than herself, and always simply ends each one with blessing and a beautiful word of prayer.

Just as Anne Hughes seems to live a life that naturally inspires whoever she may come in contact with; the same can also be said about her books. Such a talented author, both her prayer book and poems all have the same goal in mind: to help you find true happiness and the simple pleasures in life. And the same can be said about her much anticipated first novel also.

As you read this book, I sincerely hope you find the joy and happiness that Anne Hughes shows in both her actions and words and that you are inspired as I have been.

Kenya Engram

The Mystery of the Shrine Beneath

My name is Janna Ravenwood and this is my story of that spring. On Friday, April 10th, I made my way to our ancestral home, Ravenwood, along with my sisters Laura and Lisa for our father, Carl Ravenwood's, funeral. We were always a close family. My sisters and I were each two years apart and even though we quarreled when we were young, we have always been best friends. Our mother, Mae-a great beauty-died two years previously and her ashes sit on the living room mantel piece where our Dad watched over them everyday. The family dog, a sheltie named Lassie, was buried in the estate grave yard sixty-eight steps from the back gate. The house was a two story colonial with four columns on the front porch and was still quite lovely even after all these years.

I didn't know what this trip might bring. I planned to stay for some time after the funeral to prepare for the future of our family estate. I was in between jobs and life in the city had become lonely and dull. Despite the circumstances, I was glad to be going home. I needed a change, I needed a home, and I needed an adventure. Luckily I kept a journal because an adventure is what I got.

Sunday, April 12, Evening

There are many treasures in our family: Nettie, Big Ben, and James the crazy parrot. Dad's funeral was memorable. He and Mom touched many lives. The mayor and the Governor were there and the many individuals whom our parents had helped over the years. They all knew that for Dad, there was no middle ground between right and wrong. You followed your conscience. Old friends told of late night visits when Dad came up with cash to help them solve their plight. After the funeral a wonderfully strong man pulled me into his arms. It was Jeffery Krane, my high school sweetheart. I was amazed that the old chemistry was still there. He said he was studying for the priesthood but laughed and said that one beautiful lady was holding him back. I smiled.

We spent several days reminiscing, crying, and visiting with old friends. After all said their goodbyes, Laura, Lisa and I met with our family's attorney, Mr. Robert Kindle. Mr. Kindle has been our parents' attorney for as long as I can remember and is a trusted friend. He agreed to meet with me on Monday to discuss our Dad's will. We knew that the estate was split three ways-each of us girls getting an equal share of land. Since Laura and Lisa and their families live out of state, I agreed to buy out their shares and make my new home here at Ravenwood. I sent my sisters on their way and promised to keep them posted on Dad's will.

RAVEN WOOD

Anne R Hughes
8-12

Monday, April 13th

I met with Mr. Kindle today to go over Dad's will and to see if there was anything that needed to be done to finalize me taking over the estate. He said that we could take care of that business at another time but first there was something important that my Dad had left behind. Mr. Kindle handed me our family Bible and said that there was a secret letter from Dad whose contents must be guarded. As I opened the letter my heart skipped a beat. Dad had written a beautiful poem explaining that there was a family treasure, that those were not Mom's ashes on the mantle, and that there was a secret underground cavern. Dad also advised us to be vigilant because there were devious people after the treasure on the estate.

Dad's Poem:

To my darling daughters:
Your beautiful mother has been resting nearby
When I think of her I always begin to cry.

I have built an underground cavern as a shrine
And you three girls will always know what's mine.

There is a lever on lassie's headstone by the old oak tree
And by turning it a large iron plate slides free.

You will find steps leading down to some underground rooms.
Your Mother's casket is held within that tomb.

There are candle sconces all around this place
And there is so much beauty transformed in this space.

Only you can find the treasure there
And I pray you three girls will know just how much I care.

Only Big Ben knows the secret of the shrine
So tell no one of the treasures that you find.

Keep this secret safe among you three
And may this be the treasure that I foresee.

Let Big Ben take you to the tomb when night time calls
Because that is when the treasure falls.

He has been our main stay all these years
And has protected this family from our fears.

As I contemplate leaving this earth
There is one secret that needs its birth.

This secret is known only by myself and Big Ben
And as I journey to the end you need to know why and when.

Tuesday Evening, April 14th

My mind kept moving all day like a magnet back to Dad's poem. With my thoughts racing, I could not wait to explore the graveyard. I thought about Lassie's grave and that all the times I had visited it I'd never noticed a lever on the angel. With the hope building-I could not keep still. Come nightfall, I found myself at the winding stone path lined with blue spruce. After two hundred feet, the path splits left and right. The left path led to the family graveyard, the right to an old well. There, in the graveyard, stood the old oak tree with Lassie's tombstone underneath. It is an angel carved in stone with her fingers pointing down to a large metal plate on the ground. To think that all this time, I pictured Lassie's body under that plate but Dad's will said that's where the shrine could be found. I searched but there was no key, no lever, and I felt like I had let Dad down. I made my way back to my room in hopes of trying again tomorrow.

I talked to Laura and Lisa this evening about the developments since they said goodbye. I was afraid of what their advice might be-that they would rather me not pursue this adventure and to just forget about what Dad had said. I found, however, that they were more than willing to move ahead. They suggested that I talk with Big Ben and let him lead me in my next steps.

I also spoke to Mr. Kindle who called to say that the historical society wanted to declare the estate and surrounding land a public project. When Mr. Kindle refused their offer, Maxine Salmonella, the head of the society, threatened a dire circumstance if her proposal was not met. Maxine is a horrible woman with the face of a hound dog and the personality of a python. There are rumors that she comes out at night on the grounds of the estate carrying a lantern high above her head. Big Ben said he saw her wearing a hooded black robe and chanting a mantra. Rumor had it that her great ancestor was none other than Cleopatra. Because of her mischievous behaviors and her persistence, Mr. Kindle also urged me to follow Dad's instructions to search the shrine but to keep very quiet about it. He warned me not to allow Maxine to know what I was doing and to be very careful during my search.

Wednesday

Jeffrey took me to lunch and studied Dad's letter today. It seems there was a metal lever on the angel wing that when pulled down moved a heavy plate forward revealing stone steps going down to a large circular room. Dad had been adamant in stating the dangers of letting the contents of the letter fall into the wrong hands. When Jeffrey took me home he was reluctant to let me go. It was like his deep brown eyes penetrated my soul. He then pulled me into his wonderful arms and kissed me. I felt I could stay there forever. He admitted that my large breasts were still beautiful.

Thursday, April 16th

This afternoon, Big Ben knocked on my door and motioned me to come with him. He is a large man-6 foot 7-and I must admit a little slow, but he had watched over all my family for all of my life. He is a gentle giant and very protective of our family and the estate.

Ben led me out the back door through a stone path lined with Blue Spruce to a fork. We took the left path and this opened into the old family graveyard. There were many head stones. Some of the writing was barely legible. And then Ben took me to the granite angel. It was beautiful with his fingers pointing down. "Lassie Beloved" was written there.

Big Ben then took my hand and together ran it over the angel's wing until I felt a stone lever. We then pulled it down. I heard a scraping sound and a large metal plate on the ground slid back revealing stone steps leading down to a cavern underground. But as we were about to descend, we heard Nettie call for us. We quickly closed the metal plate and hurried up to the house. Nettie said that a guest had arrived. It was Maxine Salmonella the director of the Historical Society.

After I tidied up, I entered the drawing room to find Maxine snooping around. She was dressed in black. She had a deep gravelly commanding voice and told me she wanted to accomplish one thing-to buy the estate. When I told her that I was not interested she said that before we were through I would be very interested. She said I had not seen the last of her. Then she threw her head back and let out a loud cackle and stormed out of the door. When she saw James she cooed, "Sweet little bird". James loudly called back, "Ugly, ugly, ugly broad". To which she screamed, "You're just a stupid bag of feathers!" James barked, "Ugly, fat gummed pig". With this, Maxine screamed loudly and fled.

"UGLY UGLY BROOD"

Sunday, April 19th

This weekend was a busy one. Jeffrey invited me out to dinner to our favorite Italian restaurant Carlina's. I must admit I was excited at the idea of seeing this memorable man again. I took a hot bubble bath and chose a royal blue lace dress to wear. When I descended the stair case Nettie and Big Ben smiled broadly.

When the front doorbell rang Nettie opened the door with James on her shoulder. When James saw Jeffrey he sang, "Down, down, down Baby down". Jeffery laughed and we left for dinner.

I told Jeffrey I wanted him to join me on the quest to discover my mother's underground tomb. He made a commitment with me to end the evening with a search.

It was nine o'clock in the evening when Jeffrey, Big Ben and I closed the back gate and quietly began our trek. The path was lined with large stones and seven foot Blue Spruce. Soon the path split left and right and we went left to the graveyard. Ben led us to the angel headstone and gathered us around. We quickly found the stone lever and pulled it down. As we did, the metal plate on the ground made a grinding sound and slid back revealing stone steps going down with light coming from beneath. Gingerly we descended into a beautiful lighted cavern with three large rooms. In the middle of the main room was a tall marble obelisk on which was carved: "Mae my beautiful beloved-may her beauty shine forever". There was a lovely candle sconce at the base. The room to the right seemed to be the family's library which held precious jewels, Tiffany glassware, Faberge Eggs, and ancient manuscripts.

There were candle sconces that lit up the whole room, but the brightest light came from the third room and what we found left us in awe. There in the middle of the room was the coffin of my Mom made of marble with the lid in gold foil and Mom's hands closed around a long tube used for storing precious art and manuscripts.

All of this beauty was mind boggling. Then we heard muted steps on the ceiling and afraid of being discovered we quickly followed the steps up. When we closed the metal plate we saw several hooded figures in the distance chanting the mantra, "oomm oomm". We had no idea where they were going and decided it would be best to retreat to the house. As we were retreating we saw several dark hooded creatures moving to the right of us. We decided to follow them at a slow pace. All of a sudden we came upon some mounted stones in the shape of an ankh. I had read that this symbol was an Egyptian portal to Heaven. The figures were in a meditation mode calling, "oomm oomm" near the old well in a circle around the ankh. We watched in silence and after a glimpse of the leader we realized it was Maxine Salmonella. She led the group and then they began a right leg hop around the ankha and called out, "mmm mmm mmm". When we realized this was a séance of some kind and that they may be moving into a deeper mode, we became slightly frightened. We decided to head back to the house to reevaluate what we'd seen. As we were retracing out footsteps back to the house we heard James in the distance crying, "Ugly, ugly, ugly broad."

Wednesday, April 22nd

The past few days have been busy ones. Jeffrey and I spent much time in the cavern library. We mainly researched Egyptian artifacts and looked up spells on how to bring back the dead. One of the spells read:

"Come now dark spirit, reveal yourself soon
Come through the portal on this full moon."

Jeffery stated his concern as a man of God in dealing with dark forces. He gave me, Big Ben, and Nettie each a lovely pewter cross necklace to wear as our protection.

We postulated that Maxine may want to buy the estate to establish a cult there. Jeffery quoted Psalm 91 as our protection. "And He will give His angels charge over you to guide you in all your ways." We each quoted these powerful words and felt complete peace.

April 29th, Wednesday

It is now the end of April and much has been done and seen. Jeffrey and I spent a lot of time the past couple of weeks going to parties and to Carlina's for Italian cuisine. We agreed to speak nothing in public of Ravenwood and the goings on of the estate graveyard.

The old estate has really blossomed this spring. The dogwoods dressed in their white and pink, the cherry blossoms, the deep hydrangeas of blue and violet, multicolored pansies, and the heavenly scent of gardenias all give me a little pep in my step each time I walk outside. The blue spruce continues to stately line the stone path out back which leads to the graveyard and the old well.

Monday, May 4th Late

It is the first week of May and Jeffrey, Big Ben, and I set out for the shrine earlier tonight, each carrying torches. Nettie and James waited at the back door. It was nine o'clock in the evening and there was a sliver of a moon. It was a beautiful night. We again took the left path to the old graveyard. The granite angel headstone looked like she had come from Heaven. After pushing the lever, the metal floor moved back and we descended below. The candle sconces were flickering. We went immediately to the left room where Mom's coffin lay. We looked at the gold foil image again and our eyes studied the long tube her hands were holding. Jeffrey lifted it out and opened the lid. Inside was a parchment scroll. We then carefully opened it and what we saw took our breath away. The writing was in Greek. It was a love letter from Marc Antony to Queen Cleopatra from 44 BC. We guessed that this was the golden prize and must be protected. We placed the ancient tube in the house safe deep in the underground tomb until we had Mr. Kindle call in an expert to evaluate the work.

Maxine Salmonella has been making appearances and sending letters of interest to purchase Ravenwood. On her last meeting, after her offer was again turned down, she looked with piercing eyes at me and said, "On the night of the meteor passing you will die." James countered with, "Ugly, ugly, ugly broad!"

Friday May, 15th

T his week was spent with an antiquities expert named Jonas Barclay. Jonas told us that the letter was written in 44 BC in Greek. Cleopatra VII was the last of the Egyptian pharaohs and this dynasty spoke Greek instead of Egyptian because of the Hellenistic influence of Alexander the Great. As pharaoh, she consummated a liaison with Julius Caesar that solidified her grip on the throne. She aligned herself with the goddess Isis and offered sacrifices to her. She had a son by Caesar and elevated him as co-ruler. After Caesar's assassination in 44 BC, she joined forces with Marc Anthony against Caesar's legal heir Octavius who later became Augustus. After losing the Battle of Actium to Octavius, Anthony committed suicide. Cleopatra followed suit with an Asp bite on August 12 30 BC.

We sat with Mr. Barclay silently digesting the facts. He read the letter slowly which stated Antony's desire to see his beautiful love one more time before their twin suicides and stated his wish to be buried with his Queen. It was Cleopatra's intense identification with the goddess Isis and royal ties of motherhood and fertility that led the many Egyptian historians to Taposiris Magna as the probable place where the queen and Marc Antony were buried after their twin suicides.

We all noticed that there was much in the news of a comet's close passing of the Earth during the last week of May. This will be a day of much unrest.

Thursday, May 28th

Today came quickly and the speculation of the passing comet and of what its aftermath would bring has consumed the local news teams. All the news media said the moon would be full and the comet's passing at midnight would be dramatic.

Tonight at ten pm Jeffrey, Big Ben and I will set out to visit the tomb one last time.

Friday, May 29th

L ast night was lovely and fragrant. When we closed the back gate we heard the sound of drums. We followed the stone path until it turned to the right. The moon cast shadows all over and we saw twenty hooded figures circling the stone ankh and singing, "umm, umm, umm". The shadow of the well was prominent.

We each were wearing our pewter crosses. At 11:45 the group chanted:

> Come now dark goddess. Come to us soon.
> Reveal yourself to us on this powerful moon.
> We call upon you Isis bring us the Queen.
> Bring death to this daughter. Reestablish the dream.

All of a sudden a whirlwind of dark smoke arose from the crowd and the hooded figures lifted Maxine Salmonella up in the air while she cried, "Kill Janna Ravenwood!" Thin fire shot up and Jeffrey rushed this hideous figure backing her against the well and with one push the evil one fell over backward into the deep well with the black smoke following suit. In one swift moment all twenty figures scattered.

Jeffrey, Big Ben, Nettie, and I responded:

> "Lord, Bring down your angels. Banish evil this night.
> Bring faith and your justice. Bring down your light.
> Remove these times of chains of time and space.
> Send back Cleopatra-away from this place."

What we witnessed left me faint and I fell over dropping to the ground. Jeffrey lifted me up in his strong arms and held me close and said, "I'm going to insist that you marry me to keep you out of trouble. What do you say?"

I smiled.

Biography

Sometimes talents reveal themselves later in life. Anne Renfroe Hughes had always wanted to be a writer and for the past three years her dream has been a reality. She is the daughter of Carl and Mae Renfroe and sister to Jean Eickhoff and Sue Tetterton. She is the proud mother of Matt Hughes who has provided the life-like illustrations for her poetry books.

Anne received a BA in Elementary Education with a minor in English from Emory University in Atlanta, Georgia in 1966, and finished her Master's Degree in Education at the University of Georgia in 1978.

Anne was accidentally shot in 1977 which resulted in partial paralysis below the waist, but Anne did not let this get her down. Since her paralysis, Anne became 1st Runner Up and Miss Congeniality in the Miss Wheelchair Georgia Pageant and named Handicapped Woman of the Year by the Pilot Club of Georgia.

Anne is the author of "When Robins Chew Snuff" and "When Geese Circle the Moon" both books of fun poems about animals. She most recently published a prayer book entitled "Somebody Extraordinary Out There". This is her first novel.